All Dads on Deck

All Dads on Deck

JUDY DELTON

Illustrated by Alan Tiegreen

A YOUNG YEARLING BOOK

Published by
Bantam Doubleday Dell Books for Young Readers
a division of
Bantam Doubleday Dell Publishing Group, Inc.
1540 Broadway
New York, New York 10036

ISBN: 0-440-40943-8

Printed in the United States of America

June 1994

10 9 8 7 6 5 4 3 2

CWO

For Jayne Perala, and Camp Hi Ho,
with love and thanks
for being such faithful friends
of the Pee Wees

Contents

CHAPTER 1

Jody's Back!

"I want *that* cereal!" shouted Sonny Stone, grabbing the box from the grocery store shelf. "It has a free rocket ship in it!"

Sonny's mother was pushing the grocery cart with the twins in it. There was lots of apple juice and milk and baby cereal in the cart, too.

"It has too much sugar in it, Sonny," she said patiently. "It's bad for your teeth. Put it back."

Sonny lay down on the grocery store floor and kicked and screamed.

In the next aisle, Molly Duff and Mary Beth Kelly were getting grape Popsicles. It was spring, and school was just out. The weather felt hot like summer. It was time for Popsicles. Mary Beth was Molly's best friend.

"Listen!" said Mary Beth. "That sounds like Sonny screaming."

Molly listened. There was no mistaking that voice. Sonny was in the same Pee Wee Scout troop as the girls. Troop 23. They had heard his whining many times. His mother was assistant troop leader.

"He's such a baby," said Mary Beth. "He acts like he's two instead of seven."

Sonny Stone was a mama's boy. He did not have a father until last year when his mother married Larry Stone, the fire chief. They had adopted twins from another country, Lee and Lani. So Sonny now had a father and a sister and a brother. Everyone said he would not be such a baby now, but he was worse instead of better, Molly thought.

"He's more spoiled all the time," said Molly in disgust. Most of the time Molly felt sorry for Sonny because everyone picked on him and teased him. But sometimes even she got disgusted.

The girls walked around to the next aisle. Sonny was waving his arms and kicking out with his legs and screaming.

"If I were his mother, I'd be embarrassed to have a kid like that," whispered Mary Beth.

"I want that rocket ship!" Sonny yelled.

Mrs. Stone picked up the box of cereal with the rocket ship. She put it in the cart.

Molly was shocked. "He needs to be told no. He keeps getting his own way."

Sonny got up off the floor and made a face at the girls.

"How nice to see you, girls," said Mrs. Stone. "We just ran into Rachel and her father in the bread aisle."

Rachel Meyers was another Pee Wee Scout.

Molly and Mary Beth talked to the twins,

who were happy and smiling. Just as they waved bye-bye to them, a wheelchair came flying around the corner of the cereal aisle and skidded to a stop at their feet.

"Jody!" shouted Molly. "You are back in town! Are you coming to Pee Wee Scouts tomorrow?"

Jody George had a big grin on his face. He was a Pee Wee, too, but had been away on a trip with his parents. It was fun to have Jody in the troop. He let the Pee Wees ride in his wheelchair, and he had great parties at his house.

"We just got back from Florida," he said. "I'll be there."

Jody's hair was longer and his skin was tanned. Molly wished her family would travel to Florida.

Jody talked about Disney World and the rides he went on.

"I went on the roller coaster!" he said.

"In your wheelchair?" asked Mary Beth.

5

Molly and Jody laughed, and Mary Beth turned red.

"No," said Jody. "My dad carried me on."

Molly tried to think what it would feel like to be carried onto a roller coaster and a Ferris wheel and even upstairs or to the basement. Jody had a lot of fun, but it didn't make up for the fact he could not play baseball or ice-skate. But he seemed to handle that pretty well.

"Well, I gotta go. We're going to a movie. See you tomorrow."

Jody shoved off from the floor with his feet, and his chair sped down the aisle to where his dad was looking for him.

•

Sonny had opened the box of cereal and was looking for the rocket ship. Molly gave the twins a hug, and she and Mary Beth went to pay for their Popsicles.

"That's illegal, to open stuff before you pay for it," said Mary Beth. "We should report Sonny."

"His mother should say no," said Molly.

Outside, Molly's little dog Skippy was jumping up and down, waiting. He was tied to a parking meter by his red leash. Molly broke a little piece off her Popsicle and gave it to him.

He tasted it and dropped it on the sidewalk.

"It's too cold for him," said Mary Beth, laughing.

Skippy licked the purple blob slowly until it was gone.

When the girls got to Molly's house, they sat on her front steps in the spring sun. It felt warm on their hair.

"I'm so glad school is out!" said Mary Beth. "We've got all summer to just fool around."

"We won't have time to fool around," said Molly. "Tomorrow we find out what Pee Wee badge we earn next. I hope it's a fun one."

Actually, all the badges were fun, she thought. Everything she and her friends did at Scouts was fun. Singing and telling about their good deeds and going on field trips and eating Mrs. Peters's chocolate cupcakes.

What would the new badge be? Molly wondered. And what adventures did their leader have planned for them this summer? Mrs. Peters was full of surprises. Tomorrow they would find out what they were.

2

The Temporary Pee Wee

At one o'clock all the Pee Wees dashed over to Mrs. Peters's house. During the school year the meetings were at three o'clock, but now that school was out they could start earlier.

Mrs. Peters was the leader of Troop 23. The meetings were at her house. She had a husband named Mr. Peters and a baby named Nick, who were not Scouts. (Mr. Peters was too old and Nick was too young.)

Molly met Mary Beth at the corner. When they got to Mrs. Peters's house, Jody's dad was getting his wheelchair out of their car. He carried it down to Mrs. Peters's basement. Then he carried Jody down, too.

"Hello!" called their leader to Molly and Mary Beth. She put her arms around them.

"It's good to have Jody back again!" she said.

"I missed our meetings," said Jody.

Downstairs, Sonny was already sailing his plastic rocket ship over the tabletop. Rachel was there, too, and Roger White. Roger was often mean, especially to Rachel. Molly was sure there was something good about Roger. She just hadn't found out what it was yet.

Kevin Moe was reading a book, even though it was summer and he didn't have to. That's how smart Kevin is, thought Molly. Kevin wanted to be mayor of their town when he grew up. Maybe even president after that. Molly liked Kevin. She was going to marry him someday, but he didn't know it yet.

Mrs. Stone was bringing down paper plates to put their snacks on, and unfolding more chairs around the table. She stopped to give Jody a welcome-back hug.

"Are we all here?" Mrs. Peters smiled, counting noses.

The Pee Wees heard a sneeze from upstairs. "Tracy is here," said Rachel. Tracy had allergies. Behind her came Tim Noon and Lisa Ronning. They all scrambled into chairs. Jody and Kevin were playing a game of Go Fish.

"Mrs. Peters!" shouted Rachel. "Kenny and Patty Baker aren't here!"

Just as she said that, the door slammed upstairs and the Baker twins came in. They were out of breath.

"We're late because our cousin's plane was late!" shouted Kenny. His face was red.

The cousin was there. She stood between them. She had long blond hair and looked older than Pee Wee age.

"Guilty!" said this cousin, stepping forward with a big smile on her face. "My name is Ashley Baker and I'm from California. Planes are

12

always late, aren't they? In winter I stay in Florida with my grandma, but my real house is in California."

The Pee Wees stared. This cousin talked a lot. But she was glamorous. What was she doing here?

"Ashley is staying with us for the summer," said Patty. "She belongs to another Scout troop. She's just a temporary Pee Wee."

Ashley was combing her long blond hair. It looked to Molly like she might have a little lipstick on. A Pee Wee with lipstick!

Ashley had shorts on, and a red T-shirt with a sweater over her shoulders, tied by the sleeves.

"Isn't it too soon for shorts?" whispered Lisa.

"Not in California," Tracy whispered back.

Ashley flounced over to her chair and sat down at the table as if she had been coming to Mrs. Peters's house all her life.

"Well, welcome, Ashley. We are glad to have

you here. And welcome back to Jody, too! Our little troop is growing this year!"

Ashley's hand was waving. "I'm only temporary," she reminded Mrs. Peters.

"Well, you're welcome as long as you care to stay," said their leader.

Roger groaned. "We've got enough Pee Wees already," he grumbled.

Mrs. Peters glared at him.

"We want to do everything we can to make our new members welcome," she said. "It is always a good thing to bring new faces and fresh ideas into a group."

Mrs. Peters talked about past meetings and past badges. Then the Pee Wees sang the Pee Wee Song and said the Pee Wee Pledge. Then she asked if anyone had good deeds to report.

Ashley's hand shot up.

"This dude is taking over our troop," muttered Roger.

"Yes, Ashley," said Mrs. Peters.

"Mrs. Peters, I have more than one good

15

deed. Number one, I helped the movers when they packed stuff. I made sure they packed the valuable stuff in tissue paper.

"And number two, my grandma's housekeeper sprained her wrist, so it was up to me to help out."

Here Ashley sighed. "I polished the silver. That was a big job."

The Pee Wees were speechless. Who was this person with valuable things and a housekeeper?

No one else raised a hand. Molly didn't feel like telling about how she picked up doggy-doo with plastic wrap in her yard, after hearing about someone who cleaned silver and had a housekeeper.

Rachel's hand was waving.

"Mrs. Peters, I cleaned forks and spoons for my mom, too."

Finally some other Pee Wees told their good deeds. Tim said he planted tomato seeds in milk cartons, and Tracy said she made salt and pepper shakers out of her allergy-pill bottles to take camping.

"I read stories to my grandpa on our trip," said Jody.

"Well, good!" said Mrs. Peters brightly. "Those are a lot of good deeds! And now we are going to move on to our new business, which is earning a brand-new badge!"

The Pee Wees cheered and clapped. They stamped their feet, and Roger whistled through his teeth. Mrs. Peters held up her hand for silence.

"What is our new badge?" cried Mary Beth.

"It's about a holiday that is coming up soon," she said.

"Fourth of July?" shouted Roger.

"Mother's Day!" shouted Tim.

"Mother's day is past," said Ashley. "I'll bet it's Father's Day!"

"Ashley is right!" said their leader. "The holiday is Father's Day."

"How come a perfectly strange person

comes in and gets to answer our questions?" demanded Sonny. "I knew that."

Mrs. Peters frowned at Sonny, even though his mother was assistant troop leader.

"I'm going to give my dad a tie I made," said Rachel.

Before all the Pee Wees could tell about their gifts, Mrs. Peters said, "This badge won't be about gifts this year."

Roger stuck his tongue out at Rachel.

"This badge is going to be for something we are going to do for our dads. And with our dads. We are going to plan a fishing trip for Father's Day. The trip is on a Sunday. We will learn all about different kinds of fish, and about lakes and how to keep them clean. We will learn boat safety and how to bait a hook. And when we all know the rules, we will have a wonderful fishing trip with our dads."

Some of the Pee Wees cheered loudly (the ones with dads). Some of them booed (the ones without dads—and the ones who didn't like worms).

"Is there a prize for the biggest fish, Mrs. Peters?" asked Kevin.

"No, it isn't necessary to have the biggest fish. It is more important to make the holiday a good one. To get the badge, you will each learn how to fish, and try to catch one, even if it's just a small one. Now, if you are uncomfortable hooking a fish, you can draw a picture of a fish, or read about them and tell us some unusual facts."

Mrs. Peters went on to say that the Pee Wees who had no father at home could bring an uncle or a friend or a big brother in his place.

Ashley was waving her hand. She stood up and announced, "Mrs. Peters, I already have a fishing badge. I caught a marlin on my uncle's yacht."

"Rat's knees!" whispered Molly. "What's a marlin?"

"What's a yacht?" whispered Mary Beth back.

Now Rachel was on her feet. "I caught a tuna when I was in California," she said. "Can that qualify for my badge, Mrs. Peters?"

"Tuna comes in a can, not on a hook," cried Tim.

Mrs. Peters had her finger on her lips. She kept it there until everyone sat down.

"These badges will be only for fish we catch on this fishing trip," she said. "I have a list here of everything you will need to get ready for the trip. Mrs. Stone will pass the lists out. At our next meeting we will talk more about it. Now it's time for refreshments."

"Yeah!" shouted the Pee Wees. They loved cupcakes.

After they ate, they helped clean up the basement and went outside to play games until it was time to go home.

"What kind of a name is Ashley?" muttered Lisa.

"I think it's a boy's name," said Tracy.

"It can be either one," said Jody. "I saw a girl named Ashley on TV."

On the way home, Molly overheard Rachel asking Ashley about her family.

"My mom is a medical doctor," said Ashley. "An M.D. She specializes in contagious diseases."

"Like chicken pox?" squawked Sonny. "Or measles? I got shots for that stuff."

"You got shots because my mom did research on immunization."

"Pooh," said Sonny. "I don't believe it."

Ashley stamped her foot, and her blond hair swung around.

"I don't lie!" she said.

Mary Beth turned to Molly and said, "She knows more than Rachel."

Molly agreed. But was this a good thing? One know-it-all in a troop was enough. Two was going to be murder.

CHAPTER 3

Hooks, Lines, and Sinkers

"I hear you and I have a big Father's Day fishing trip coming up!" said Mr. Duff at supper.

"How did you know?" asked Molly. "We just found out!"

"Mrs. Peters called all of the parents to get permission," said Mrs. Duff, passing Molly the pasta salad. "We all will help get the equipment ready."

"We get a fishing badge," said Molly. "We have to catch a fish."

"I intend to catch the biggest fish in the lake," said Molly's dad. "A shark."

"There are no sharks in our lakes." Molly laughed.

"In any lake," agreed her mother. "Sharks are in the ocean."

"It isn't the size that matters anyway," said Molly. "We don't need a big, big fish to get our badge. Any fish will do."

"A goldfish?" asked Mr. Duff.

Molly wrinkled her nose at her father and made a face. She knew he was kidding.

"Do I get a badge, too?" asked Mr. Duff.

Molly laughed at the picture of her dad wearing a badge.

"You're too old," she said.

At the next meeting, the first thing Mrs. Peters did was talk about water safety.

"We will rent a small launch," she said. "That way we can all be on the same boat. A regular rowboat only holds four. And you cannot stand up in a rowboat. In a launch we can walk around and stretch our legs. And we can all be together. Everyone must be sure to wear a safety jacket at all times."

Mrs. Peters held up an orange vest with ties down the front.

"Mrs. Peters?" called Ashley, her hand waving. "We have a boat. We could all use that and we wouldn't have to rent one."

"Your boat is in California," said Kenny. "What good would it do us there?"

"Oh, that's right," said Ashley, sitting down.

After everyone looked at the vest and tried it on, Mrs. Peters talked about boat behavior and fishing poles and rods and reels.

"And we all must wear hats for the sun," she said. "It can get hot out on the lake, even in spring."

"What about food?" asked Sonny. "I don't want to starve to death out on that lake."

Now the Pee Wees frowned.

"What if the engine conks out and we're shipwrecked on a desert island?" asked Tracy.

"Hey, you'd have to eat plants and ants and stuff," said Roger.

"I'm allergic to plants," said Tracy.

"What if there is a storm and the boat tips over?" yelled Tim.

"Or we lose the anchor and drift too far out?" said Patty.

"We could camp out and live like Gilligan," said Kevin. "Or Robinson Crusoe."

Suddenly the fun fishing trip was turning into a dangerous adventure, thought Molly.

"Nothing like that will happen," said Mrs. Peters. "The lake is not like the ocean, you know. We will have picnic hampers full of food. And cold drinks in the cooler. There will be a man to run the boat who knows all about it. There will be safety rafts just in case."

"In case of what?" cried Sonny. "I don't want to be on a raft with all those sharks with the sharp teeth."

Sonny's face got red, and he looked as if he were going to cry.

"There are no sharks!" said Mrs. Peters firmly.

Roger was under the table, pretending to be a shark, nipping at knees, and pinching Sonny. "Grrrr," he said.

"Sharks don't growl," said Jody, laughing, and he grabbed Roger's head.

"We will make a trip to the bait store to learn about fishing poles and hooks and lines and sinkers," said Mrs. Peters.

"I have my own bobbers and sinkers," said Jody. "From last summer when I went with my uncle."

"Mrs. Peters, are we going to fly-fish?" asked Rachel. "My grandpa does that."

"Who wants to fish for flies?" asked Tim. "You can catch flies in a jar, or hit them with a flyswatter."

Mrs. Peters explained that fly-fishing was not catching flies.

"We are just going to drop our line in the lake with bait on it, and a sinker and bobber," she said. "A bobber floats on the water, and when it goes down, a fish is on the line and you pull it in."

"I can cast," said Roger. He ran around the room, casting with a make-believe rod and reel.

"I had a cast on my leg once," said Mary Beth. "I hope it's not that kind of a cast."

"I went to a cast party when I was in *Cinderella*!" said Tracy.

"We are not casting," said Mrs. Peters, frowning at Roger. "Casting is when you throw the line away from the shore, and it is done mostly in rivers."

"Who's going to take the fish off the hook?" asked Patty.

"I am sure your dads will do that, and show you how, too," she said.

Mrs. Peters held up a book with a picture of a lady taking the hook out of a fish's mouth.

"You back the hook up so that the prongs slide out," said Mrs. Peters. She had a real hook in her hand to show them.

"Doesn't that hurt the fish?" cried Molly.

"A little," said their leader. "But fish have few nerves in their body."

Molly could not believe that it didn't hurt the fish a lot. Mrs. Stone was passing out cookies, but Molly didn't take any.

After the meeting, the Pee Wees stopped at the park and sat on a bench in the sun.

"That's lipstick Ashley has on, I know it is," said Mary Beth. "My mom wouldn't let me wear that stuff, especially to Scouts."

"She looks like she's in fifth grade or something," agreed Tracy.

"I'm not going to catch my fish with a hook," said Molly.

The Pee Wees looked at her.

"How are you going to catch it?" asked Mary Beth.

31

"I don't know yet," said Molly. "But I know a hook must hurt the fish's mouth."

"Naw," said Roger. "Fish don't feel anything."

"How would you like it if someone caught *you* on a hook, Roger White?" said Rachel. "Would you like a hook in your mouth?"

"I'm not a fish!" said Roger.

"Well, Mrs. Peters said we don't have to catch a fish to get the badge," said Mary Beth. "You can draw a fish or read about a fish instead."

"I don't want to read about them or draw them!" said Molly. "I want to go on the trip and fish with everyone else. I just don't want to hurt the fish."

Molly sighed. Father's Day wasn't even here yet, and already she had a problem. Was she the only one who worried about a fish's health? Would she be the only one at home reading and drawing instead of fishing on the lake?

CHAPTER 4

No Hook for Molly

On Wednesday there was a special meeting of the Pee Wees so that they could take a tour of the bait store. When they went in, they saw tanks and tanks of small fish swimming around and through green weeds.

"Hey, we could catch these fish with a little net!" shouted Sonny.

"But they are too small to fry, aren't they, Mrs. Peters?" asked Mary Beth.

"These fish are minnows," said their leader. "They are the bait we use to get bigger fish."

The Pee Wees leaned over the tanks and watched them swim. The man who owned the shop picked one up and put it on a hook. Then he dropped the hook in the water.

"When a big fish comes along, he grabs the minnow in his mouth and gets hooked. Then you pull him up and have him for dinner!" he said.

To catch a fish, you had to hurt *two* fishes instead of one, thought Molly. Now she definitely did not want to catch a fish with a hook. There had to be another way—a nicer way to catch a fish.

The man walked over to the counter where there were little plastic containers of worms. They looked like the containers in Molly's refrigerator that held cottage cheese or leftover spaghetti.

"You just slide the worm on the hook like this," he said, demonstrating for the Pee Wees.

Molly quivered. This wasn't getting any better.

"Let me do it!" shouted Roger.

All the boys wanted to bait hooks. Even Rachel and Tracy and Lisa wanted to. No one in this group was going to draw or read instead of fish.

"Ouch!" cried Sonny. "That worm bit me!"

"Worms don't bite, dummy." Roger laughed.

But Sonny was crying and holding up his finger. It did have a red mark on it. His mother took a Band-Aid out of her purse and put it on his finger.

"The hook probably stuck him," said Rachel.

Mr. Olson, the owner, showed the Pee Wees tackle boxes and fishing line and bobbers and sinkers. He showed them fishing hats and lunch boxes and rubber rafts and safety jackets. There were pillows to put on the boat seats and nets to land big fish in, and even some boats and oars for sale.

"We don't need most of these things," said Mrs. Stone. "And we already have most of what we need."

Even so, Lisa bought a fishing hat that said THE BIG ONE GOT AWAY.

Ashley bought a straw basket called a "creel" to keep her fish in.

And Mrs. Peters bought a minnow pail.

"We'll get the minnows and worms on Sunday morning," she said.

Mr. Olson talked about fishing safety and water pollution.

"Don't throw any litter into a lake," he said. "And be sure no oil leaks from your motor into the water."

"We better check that guy's motor," said Kenny. "What if we pollute?"

"We will leave that up to the owner of the boat," said Mrs. Peters. "He or she will not want us checking the motor."

"The best fishing is in the early morning around five o'clock, when the fish are hungry,"

Mr. Olson went on. "And then at supper-time."

"Do the fish eat meals at the same time we do, Mr. Olson?" asked Tim.

Everyone laughed.

"Well, they get hungry when they wake up, just like you. And by evening they are hungry again after all that swimming."

Molly wrote that down in the notebook she was carrying with her. She had an idea. An idea of how to keep the fish from getting hurt.

But how could she catch a fish without a hook? Would she have to get her badge the boring way and miss the fishing trip?

No one else seemed to mind those sharp hooks. She decided not to tell anyone her plan right now. They wouldn't understand, and they would all laugh at her.

Now all the Pee Wees were lined up in front of lures.

"These lures are artificial bait," said Mr. Olson. He held one up. It was red and blue and green and purple. It was bright and flashy and had feathers on it, and metal disks that shone in the light.

"The sun catches these and it attracts the fish," he said. "They swim toward it and get themselves hooked."

All the lures were in a glass case. Each one was in a little box. They all had lots of hooks hidden in their feathers, not just one. And they were big hooks.

"I want one of those!" shouted Roger. "I can catch a giant fish with that."

"They are used for trolling," said Mr. Olson.

"What's trolling?" whispered Mary Beth to Molly.

"I'll bet you put one of those troll dolls on your line along with the lure," said Tracy. "I've got one with red hair. I can bring it."

"I think you are better off with live bait in our lakes," said Mr. Olson. "But some people do make their own lures. Smaller ones than these. I have some things here to make your own artificial bait." He moved to another counter.

Some of the Pee Wees bought little feathers and sequins to make their own lures.

But Molly did not want to make artificial bait.

She wanted to make an artificial FISH!

If only she could make a fish that looked real enough so that she could get her badge without using a hook. But Mrs. Peters would know the difference between a real fish and one Molly made out of clay or cardboard. Mrs. Peters was smart. She wasn't Scout leader for nothing.

No, Molly would have to think of another way. What in the world would it be?

CHAPTER 5

Fish Food

"Well, it won't be long now," said Mr. Duff at breakfast the next morning. "I've got my tackle ready to go."

Rat's knees. Now would be the time for Molly to tell her dad her worry, she thought. But if she did, it might ruin Father's Day. It was no fun to have someone along on a fishing trip who did not want to catch a fish.

It seemed to Molly that her father should be more sensitive. He wouldn't let her hurt little Skippy. Why, he didn't even step on ants when he walked! Why didn't he care about fish?

But she just said, "Good!" to her dad.

Then she excused herself to go to Mary Beth's.

Mr. Kelly was going out the door to work when she got there.

"So the big day is coming up!" he said to Molly. "I got a new rod and reel for my birthday I'm dying to use!"

"Good," said Molly. It was the second time already this morning she had said "good" when she meant "bad."

The girls rode their bikes around the park. Roger was there, digging in the dirt.

"You aren't supposed to dig in the park," said Mary Beth.

"I'm digging my own worms. My dad says we can save money bringing our own bait."

"I'm not going to use bait," Molly confided to Mary Beth when they got back home.

"Fish won't bite on a bare hook," Mary Beth said.

"I'm not going to use a hook," said Molly.

Mary Beth stared at her. "Well, no fish is going to jump out of the water into your lap!" she said.

"I might buy my fish," said Molly.

"That's not fair!" said Mary Beth. "That won't count."

"No one will know," said Molly. "I'll bring it along and tie it on my line."

Buying a fish would solve the whole hook problem. She would fish without a hook, and then when no one was looking she would pull her line up and pretend the store fish was the one she caught! She couldn't buy it yet because fish need refrigeration. And if she put it in the refrigerator at home, her mother would ask questions.

Molly went home and counted her money. She put all the money from her piggy bank into her purse.

The day before the fishing trip, Molly went to the grocery store. She went to the meat section. She looked at rows and rows of pork chops. And rows and rows of hamburger and steaks. A whole case was full of chickens. Finally she saw the fish.

But they all had their heads cut off! If she caught a fish with no head, Mrs. Peters and her dad would be suspicious.

Then she saw some fish with their heads on. They were on a bed of ice in a special case. They had a body that looked scaly, or like a shell. They even had tails. The sign said FRESH JUMBO SHRIMP.

"I'll have one of those, please," said Molly.

"Just one?" asked the butcher, with a smile. "Do you want some seafood dip to go with it?"

"No, thank you," said Molly. "I'm not going to eat it. I'm going to catch it."

The butcher looked surprised, but he didn't ask any more questions. He wrapped the shrimp in some white paper and wrote "$1.05" on it and handed it to Molly. Molly had a little money left over, so she stopped in the bakery department and bought a big bag of donuts. She had another idea.

Molly put the fish under her bed for the night. Now at last she could have a good time on the fishing trip, too! Without hurting a single fish herself! Buying one already dead didn't count, she thought.

The next morning she heard her dad up early.

"Happy Father's Day!" she called.

"Well, you're in a good mood today," said her dad. He looked relieved.

"I am," said Molly.

She pulled her jeans on and washed her face and brushed her teeth and combed her hair.

Something smelled bad. What in the world was it?

Then she knew. It was her fish! It was not cool under her bed.

She put the package of fish and the package of donuts into her tote bag. Her dad had all the fishing equipment ready.

Molly and her dad drove over to the Peterses' house. When they got out of the car, the Bakers drove up. Everything Ashley wore had a nautical theme. Even her tote bag had a fish on it.

Rachel and her dad were waiting with their equipment.

"Phew, what smells around here?" shouted Roger, looking at Molly.

"I think it's your tote bag," said Mary Beth. She looked into the bag.

Rat's knees! Why hadn't Molly put that fish in a Ziploc bag?

"Why are you bringing donuts?" she asked. "We get lunch on the boat."

"Shh," whispered Molly. "They are for the fish."

"We're supposed to catch the fish, not feed them!" said her friend.

"Mrs. Peters said the fish were hungry in the morning," said Molly.

"They will eat the worms on our hooks," said Mary Beth. Then she walked over to look at Tracy's fishing pole.

The fish wouldn't eat the worms on the hooks if Molly had anything to say about it. If she fed them first, they might turn their noses up at the worms on the hidden hooks and swim away. The donuts were far better-tasting than worms. They were chocolate and had frosting with little sprinkles. She would be able to protect not only her own fish but all the other fish, too!

The Pee Wees piled into the vans with their dads and buckled their seat belts.

"Here we go!" shouted Roger. "Watch out, giant fish, I'm going to get you!"

Not if I can help it, thought Molly.

The dads and the uncles laughed and joked. Jody's wheelchair was folded and tied to the top of the van.

Tim was pretending he was a fish and was using his arms for fins.

His uncle Roy pretended to swim after him. "Got you!" he yelled, making Tim giggle.

"We have a wonderful day for the trip!" said Mr. Peters. "Just look at that sun! It's a perfect Father's Day."

"We won't know if it's perfect till we see how many fish we get," said Roger's dad with a laugh.

Kevin's dad was passing out flyers to all the other dads. The flyers said VOTE FOR MOE FOR SCHOOL BOARD.

He told them all the changes that needed to be made by the school board. He told them about one school that was overcrowded.

"And that's why I'm running for school board," he said.

"No wonder Kevin is such a politician!" whispered Mary Beth to Molly.

Finally they got to the lake, and the launch was waiting.

"All dads on deck!" called Mrs. Peters, laughing. "And uncles, too!"

Hank, the man in charge of the launch, helped them load their things aboard. Then he told them about the safety rafts lined up on the deck, and how to press a red button to inflate them in case of emergency.

"But we probably won't ever need those," he said, and he smiled.

All the Pee Wees smiled, too, except Sonny.

"It's not funny," he said. "I don't want to be sitting on one of those things out there." He looked over the railing at the water. The wind was blowing, and the water was wavy.

"How deep is it?" he asked Hank.

"It's good and deep out there where we get the pike," Hank said cheerfully. "Way over your head, little guy."

That was not the thing to tell Sonny.

He burst into tears and wanted to go home. Nothing Larry said seemed to quiet him.

"What a baby," said Ashley. "Is he going to cry the whole trip and ruin it?"

Mr. George helped Jody settle in a deck chair along the railing. While everyone went exploring the boat, Molly sat down beside Jody.

Now that Mary Beth had noticed the donuts, she was worried that someone else might, too.

All of a sudden she burst out and told Jody her worries. And how Mary Beth had found the donuts. When she was finished, Jody said, "I don't want to hurt the fish, either. But I thought I was the only one. I think the donuts are a great idea! I can keep them under my chair here till the time is right."

"Really?" shrieked Molly. She reached into her bag and handed him the donuts.

The Pee Wees came back and ran around the deck.

"I'll watch for the right chance," he said. "When no one is looking."

Molly felt good, knowing someone else felt the same way she did. Not even her best friend, Mary Beth, seemed to understand.

Just then Mr. Duff came looking for Molly. Hank was taking a group below the deck to the galley, or tiny kitchen.

"Look, there's even a little refrigerator!" said Tracy.

"We have one of those on our boat, too," said Ashley.

That is where my fish should be, thought Molly. But there was no way to put it there without being seen.

Hank showed them where the engine was, and then made sure everyone's life jacket was tied.

Then he untied the launch from the dock and

started the boat. The engine roared, the water parted, and their boat sped off.

"Yippee!" shouted the Pee Wees. Troop 23 was asea!

CHAPTER 6

Donuts and Shrimp

When they got to the place where the fish were hungry, Hank turned off the engine and dropped the anchor. Mr. and Mrs. Peters went around and helped bait hooks. Some Pee Wees and their dads used worms, some minnows, and some used the bait they had made. Lisa's dad had bait that looked like a bug. "My dad made it," she said proudly.

Larry Stone put bobbers and sinkers on some of the lines. The dads put them on others. Rachel and Kevin put their own bait on.

"Yuck!" said Ashley. "I'm not touching any dirty old worm."

"I feel the same way," said Mr. Baker. "You and I can stick to lures."

Molly wondered how she was going to get the hook off her line. Her dad had just put it on. Then Mr. Duff walked over to talk to Mr. White. Molly quickly pulled her line up and untied the hook. She took it off and she left the bobber and the sinker on. Then she threw the baitless line back in the water.

"Where are the fish?" demanded Sonny.

"Fish don't bite that fast, young man," said Hank. "You have to have patience to be a fisherman."

The Pee Wees sat with their lines in the water. They watched their bobbers.

It was quiet, and the water lapped the sides of the boat gently. The air smelled fresh (except near Molly's tote bag). Molly watched Jody for a sign that it was safe to get the donuts. And she wondered how she could get her shrimp fish tied on to her hook when she pulled it up.

It didn't take long till her chance came. She heard Jody whistle. She went over to his chair, and he said, "Nobody's in the front of the boat. It's safe to feed the fish up there."

Molly looked. He was right. And her dad was taking some seaweed off Kenny's line. Molly put her pole down and took the donuts Jody handed her. She walked around past the life rafts. No one could see her. Jody winked and nodded.

She took out the donuts and broke them up into small pieces and threw them over the railing. Several fish appeared and grabbed them! It was working!

She saw Jody toss some pieces from his chair when no one was looking, too.

Just as she was about to throw the last donut piece overboard, Sonny yelled:

"What are you doing? What are you throwing overboard?"

Sonny had popped up from nowhere. He

must have come from the other direction! Even Jody had not seen him.

Sonny saw the donut in her hand.

"I'm just giving the fish a little treat," said Molly, feeling like a criminal.

Sonny looked over the railing. Lots of fish were eating now.

Sonny ran back to the group, shouting, "Molly's feeding the fish! They are all eating donuts!"

Rat's knees! Sonny was a tattletale. Why couldn't he keep anything to himself?

Now Roger was taking up the refrain. "Now the fish won't want our bait, dummy!" He leaned over the railing and looked at the fish gobbling up the donuts.

"It's all right," whispered Jody to Molly. "Those fish are full now. They aren't going to want any worms for a long time!"

Hank tried to make Molly feel better. "These fish have big appetites," he said. But that is exactly what Molly did not want to hear.

Molly's dad looked puzzled.

For a long time no fish bit their bait. They sat for half an hour without a nibble.

"See?" said Jody. "It worked! Those fish are full!"

"It's Molly's fault," growled Roger.

Hank took up the anchor and moved the boat to another spot.

He's going where there are new fish, thought Molly. Hungry fish.

She was right. Before long Tim's bobber went underwater.

"Pull it in!" shouted his uncle Roy.

Mr. Peters grabbed his pole to help.

Tracy's dad got the net ready.

"Yea for Tim!" called Mrs. Peters. "He got the first fish!"

The fish was a sunfish. Molly did not watch as Tim's uncle Roy took the hook out of its mouth and put it in a pail of water.

One by one the Pee Wees caught fish. Hank got a walleye. And Sonny got a bullhead with black whiskers sticking out all over its round head.

"Hey, Stone's fish looks just like *him*!" shouted Roger.

Sonny gave him a kick.

"Psst," said Jody to Molly. "I took the hook off my line. No fish is going to get his mouth hurt on *my* line!"

"But you won't get a badge!" said Molly.

"I'll draw a picture of a fish," Jody said, and shrugged.

Jody was brave! He wasn't afraid to stand up for his rights.

Molly felt very close to him. Maybe she would marry Jody instead of Kevin! She wasn't sure she wanted to marry a mayor anyway.

Pretty soon Mary Beth got a little crappie that had to be thrown back because it was too small to eat.

"But it still counts," said Mrs. Peters.

Mary Beth took it off the line herself, with her dad's glove on.

Molly decided she would have to get that shrimp on her line soon or risk not getting a badge. No fish would get caught on a hookless line. And Molly did not want it to.

"Did you check your bait, Molly?" asked her dad. "Maybe the fish nibbled it off."

"I will," said Molly quickly. "I can do it myself."

She walked over to a life raft and pulled her line up. She bent down and quickly tied her line around the shrimp's waist. She popped it back in the water. It got tangled up on the end of the boat, but then it sunk.

All of a sudden her bobber went underwater! She had not thought of this! What if some big fish was eating her shrimp? She would be without a badge after all her work! The line went down again and bent her pole in half.

65

Either a big fish was there, or her shrimp had gained a lot of weight.

"I think you've got your fish!" said Mr. Duff in great excitement. "I was afraid you were never going to catch one!"

At least her fish wasn't a lie. She DID have a fish on her line!

But what was pulling it down in the water so hard?

All the men sprang over to help Molly land her fish. The net was ready. Up, up, up, up. And finally there was her fish, sparkling in the sunlight.

"It's an old pail!" shouted Kenny. "A pail full of water! And a bunch of seaweed!"

Sure enough, Molly's line had got twisted around some seaweed and onto the handle of an old pail.

As her dad grabbed the pail, she asked, "Don't I have a fish on my line?"

"Let's see," said her dad. He peered in the pail. There was Molly's shrimp, still tied

to her line. Limp and wet, but it was there!

"I caught a fish!" shrieked Molly.

Everyone gathered around to see it. They stared.

"What the heck is it?" asked Lisa.

"That's no fish," said Sonny. "It looks like a worm!"

"It's no worm!" said Molly, stamping her foot.

Ashley peered at the line. "It's a *shrimp*!" she shouted. "How could you catch a shrimp in a lake? Shrimp live in the ocean!"

Molly hadn't known that. A fish was a fish, she had thought. Now she realized her mistake. Shrimp must come from salt water!

"Why did you buy a *shrimp*?" whispered Mary Beth.

Molly felt embarrassed. "The others had their heads off," she told her. "It's a fish, and I caught it," she said. "What's the difference what kind it is?"

68

Mrs. Peters threw back her head and roared. "I think I know what happened," she said.

"So do I," said Molly's dad, putting an arm around his daughter.

"I didn't want to hurt a fish with a hook," Molly blurted out.

Mrs. Peters gave Molly a hug. "There is nothing wrong with thinking about the fish's feelings," she said. "There are lots and lots of people who do not fish or hunt because they do not believe in hurting animals."

Molly's dad took her aside and said, "You didn't have to go out and buy a fish, honey. You could have told me how you felt. Remember, you can't let anyone force you to do something you don't believe in."

Molly was very glad to hear her father say that. She felt a flood of relief now that her dad knew! It was no fun to keep secrets from your family, she thought.

"I didn't want to ruin the party," said Molly.

Molly's dad was just about to empty the old pail into the lake when he discovered something.

"Look!" he said. "There is a fish in this pail! And it is not a shrimp!"

The Pee Wees looked. There in the water in the pail was a small sunfish!

"I did catch a fish!" shouted Molly. "Without a hook!"

Everyone laughed.

"Molly caught two fish, instead of one," said Mrs. Peters.

"This one counts as Jody's fish," said Molly, smiling at Jody. "He didn't want to hurt a fish, either," she explained to her dad.

The fish flopped in the pail.

"Do we have to keep it?" asked Molly.

"Let's put it back in the water," said Molly's dad.

Molly felt relieved.

"I caught a fish," said Jody, "and we didn't even have to hurt it!"

Together Molly and her dad emptied the pail over the railing.

"Now I know just how I'll draw my fish," said Jody.

CHAPTER 7

Emergency!

After everyone had caught a fish, and some of the dads three or four, Ashley came up to Molly. She put her arm through Molly's and said, "I think it is great you don't want to hurt fish. You're a nice person."

Molly was surprised. Just when she decided Ashley was a show-off, she said something kind. It helped to have others feel the same as she did! And Ashley liked her!

"My grandma is a vegetarian," Ashley went on. "She doesn't eat any meat or any fish."

"My aunt doesn't eat anything 'with a face,'" said Jody. "She eats Chinese stir-fry with cabbage and tofu and stuff."

"Hey, cabbage has a face!" said Roger.

"Does not, dum dum," said Rachel.

"Does, too," said Roger.

Soon the Pee Wees were all taking sides about whether vegetables and fruit had faces.

"A pumpkin does!" said Tim. "At Halloween!"

Mrs. Peters had to hold up her hand for silence, just as she did at the meetings.

"We'll be having a good Father's Day luncheon here on the deck in a little while," she said. "First we will put all of our fishing equipment away like good Scouts."

The dads and the Scouts rinsed off the hooks. They wound up the fishing lines. They put the sinkers and bobbers in the right place in the tackle boxes. They put the covers on the cans of worms. And Hank swept some of the fishy water from the deck into the lake.

The Pee Wees stretched out in folding chairs to rest. The water was blue. The sky was blue.

And all the trees along the shore were bursting into new green leaves. The water lapped, lapped, lapped at the side of the boat. It was so peaceful, Molly thought she could almost fall asleep. But in the background she could hear Roger's father.

"I built a boat myself," he said. "From scratch."

He sounds just like Roger, thought Molly.

"You're welcome to come over and see it, Meyers," Mr. White said.

Molly opened one eye. She saw Mr. White give Rachel's dad a punch on the arm. He acts just like Roger, too! thought Molly.

"I'll do that," said Rachel's dad.

"Maybe we can take the kids for a spin some weekend, and try it out."

"That's a good idea. Maybe over the Fourth of July."

Molly couldn't believe what she was hearing! If Mr. White and Dr. Meyers got to be friends, Rachel and Roger would be going boating together! Molly looked around. Rachel and Roger were not there. They had not heard this new plan. And Molly didn't want to be around when they did!

"Mrs. Peters, can I take off my safety vest?" asked Ashley. "It's all lumpy and uncomfortable. And orange isn't my color."

"I'm sorry, Ashley, but we have to wear our life jackets while we are on the water."

"I can swim," said Ashley, pouting.

"A person may be too nervous to swim," said Mrs. Peters. "We have the jackets in case of emergency."

Sonny was farther down on the deck. He heard the word "emergency," but he didn't hear the words "in case of."

"Emergency!" he screamed, and ran like a shot to the life rafts. Before anyone could get there, he had pressed the red buttons. From one to the other he ran, inflating the rafts.

"Come on!" he yelled. "Help me get these overboard."

But Sonny could not lift the inflated rafts! They were huge and they were clumsy. When they got to their full size, they took up almost the whole deck! The Pee Wees could hardly move!

"What's the emergency?" called Hank, running up from the galley.

"Is there a man overboard?" yelled Roger, leaning over the railing.

Mr. Peters was walking in and out between the rafts, counting noses.

"I think we are all here," he said.

"I'll bet there's a leak in the boat!" said Sonny. "Look at the water up front!"

"That's no leak, dummy," said Roger. "It's from splashing water."

"Well, there's some emergency, I heard somebody say so," said Sonny.

The dads covered the whole boat. They did not find an emergency.

The Pee Wees were squished against the railing because of the inflated rafts.

"Who did this?" asked Hank. "Who inflated these rafts?"

The Pee Wees pointed to Sonny. He was hiding under one of the rafts.

"I saw him," said Ashley. "I was talking to Mrs. Peters about taking off my life jacket, and she said we need it in case of emergency, and then Sonny ran and pressed all those red buttons."

Larry Stone scratched his head. "Somehow I knew Sonny was at the bottom of all of this," he said.

Sonny peeked out from under a raft. Larry brought him out. Sonny was crying.

Mrs. Peters put her arm around Sonny and said, "No harm done. The one thing we can all be grateful for is there is no real emergency."

Mrs. Peters was too nice, thought Molly. She should have pounded Sonny.

"Well, now that the rafts are inflated, we

may as well turn them over and use them for picnic tables!" said Hank, laughing.

"Baby," said Rachel to Sonny as she and Tracy and Lisa set a paper plate for each person on the rafts.

"We needed tables anyway." Sonny pouted.

"Yeah, Stone, sure! Like you knew what you were doing," said Roger.

Hank and Mrs. Peters and Mr. Peters carried in the food. On a little folding table was a big cake. It had blue frosting for the lake. On the blue lake was a small boat. It had a flag on it that said PEE WEES. Around the edges were frosting fish in all shapes. And across the sky, frosting letters said HAPPY FATHER'S DAY, DADS!

"It's too pretty to eat," said Tracy.

"Our cook makes cakes like this," said Ashley. "Every year on my birthday. Only it says HAPPY BIRTHDAY TO ASHLEY instead of HAPPY FATHER'S DAY, and sometimes it has my horse on it."

The Pee Wees scrambled around the rafts.

They were all hungry from the fresh air and exercise. They ate all the food there, and more food when it was brought in.

They ate sandwiches and potato salad and watermelon and pickles. They drank milk and soda pop and fruit juice.

"Save room for the cake!" warned Mrs. Peters.

The Pee Wees did. Then they sang "Happy Father's Day" to the dads, to the tune of "Happy Birthday." They sang the Pee Wee Song and said the Pee Wee Pledge.

After they helped carry away the trash, the dads told stories about other fishing trips. And some of them told stories about sailing.

"I remember a canoe trip when the rapids were so strong we almost went over the falls," said Mr. George. "The water swept our lunch and even our shoes out of the boat and down the river."

"Where do you canoe?" asked Tim's uncle Roy.

"We usually go to the Bush River," answered Mr. George.

"I go there, too!" said Roy.

"We're going next weekend. Why don't you and Tim come along?"

"Great," said Roy, making a note in a small notebook he carried in his shirt pocket.

Tim looked pleased, thought Molly. What a good Father's Day this was.

When the Pee Wees could hardly keep their eyes open any longer, Hank pulled the anchor up and headed the boat toward shore. They piled off the boat and into the vans.

"Thank you, Hank," they called as they waved good-bye.

"I feel seasick," said Sonny, holding his stomach.

"How can you be seasick on dry land?" asked Mary Beth.

But Sonny was, and Larry picked him up and wrapped him in some jackets, and then held him on his lap.

83

"Too much excitement in one day," said Larry.

"Boy, I'd hate to be Sonny's father," said Ashley.

"If I were Larry, I'd put Sonny up for adoption and keep the twins," said Lisa.

The vans came to a stop at the Peterses' house, and each of the dads (or uncles) found his own Pee Wee and drove home, with their fish and their happy memories.

Just as the Meyers' car passed Molly's, Molly heard Rachel scream, "No way!"

Her dad must have told her about the Whites, thought Molly, smiling. Wait till Roger heard the news! Molly couldn't wait till next Tuesday for their Pee Wee meeting!

When they got home, Mrs. Duff was waiting to hear about the trip.

"I had a great time!" said Mr. Duff to his wife. "We have lots of stories to tell you."

They told her about the inflatable rafts. And

about Molly's catch. And about the good lunch and the fancy cake.

Molly wished she could tumble into bed with all of her clothes on. But she smelled fishy. She needed a bath first.

When she had her pajamas on, she crawled into bed and pulled her clean sheets up to her chin. She felt happy all over. She had had a good time with her dad on Father's Day. She had "caught" two fish. She had gotten to know Jody better. And maybe she would have a new friend in Ashley. Besides that, some Pee Wee dads had become friends. "All this and badges too!" she said as she turned out the light. Rat's knees, it was fun to be a Pee Wee!

Pee Wee Scout Song

(to the tune of
"Old MacDonald Had a Farm")

Scouts are helpers, Scouts have fun
Pee Wee, Pee Wee Scouts!
We sing and play when work is done,
Pee Wee, Pee Wee Scouts!

With a good deed here,
And an errand there,
Here a hand, there a hand,
Everywhere a good hand.

Scouts are helpers, Scouts have fun,
Pee Wee, Pee Wee Scouts!

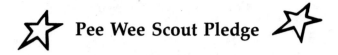 **Pee Wee Scout Pledge**

We love our country
And our home,
Our school and neighbors too.

As Pee Wee Scouts
We pledge our best
In everything we do.